**Collins**

Scary Play

by
Judith Johnson

Resource Material by
Anthony Banks
and
Suzy Graham-Adriani

William Collins' dream of knowledge for all began with the publication of his first book in 1819. A self-educated mill worker, he not only enriched millions of lives, but also founded a flourishing publishing house. Today, staying true to this spirit, Collins books are packed with inspiration, innovation and a practical expertise. They place you at the centre of a world of possibility and give you exactly what you need to explore it.

Collins. Do more.

Published by Collins
An imprint of HarperCollins*Publishers*
77–85 Fulham Palace Road
Hammersmith
London
W6 8JB

Commissioned by Charlie Evans
Design by JPD
Cover design by Charlotte Wilkinson
Production by Simon Moore
Printed and bound by Martins the Printers Ltd

Browse the complete Collins catalogue at www.collinseducation.com

Acknowledgements

Photo credits: Alamy, pp77, 79; DHA Lighting / Rosco, p80; Getty Images, cover, pp77, 78, 90; Simon Annand, pp76, 89.

Text credits: pp94-5 extract from Darren Shan, *Hunters of the Dusk: Vampires at War* is reproduced with the permission of HarperCollins *Publishers*.

Playscript copyright © Judith Johnson 2007.

10 9 8 7 6 5 4

ISBN-13 978-0-00-725489-7
ISBN-10 0-00-725489-X

British Library Cataloguing in Publication Data

A Catalogue record for this publication is available from the British Library

Contents

PLAYSCRIPT

The Writer

Judith Johnson has now been writing for nearly twenty years! She has written stage plays for the National, Royal Court, Liverpool Playhouse and Everyman, English Touring Theatre, Chelsea Theatre and Arcola Theatre amongst others. She has also written for radio and TV. *Scary Play* is her third Connections Play. *Stone Moon* was commissioned for the very first Connections Scheme, *The Willow Pattern* (full length and Assembly versions) followed in 2004. She is currently working on a radio play, a musical and two new stage plays.

Characters

KAL   10 years old. Clever and tough. Or so he thinks anyway. Prone to telling the odd porky.

MAL   Also 10. Kal's best mate. Daft as a brush.

RO   Short for Romeo. Also 10. The best looking boy in the class. Or, at the very least, the one with the best clothes and largest amount of hair gel.

TILLY   Also 10. Very girly. Very pretty. Ro's girlfriend.

JAZ   Tilly's best friend. Also 10. Smart and feisty.

BOFF   10. Clever and not tough. Very sweet but very anxious.

LOU   Kal's sister. 8 years old. Thinks she's a boy.

THE MAN   Grown up. Could be anything from 18–80. Calm and polite on the surface, a seething pit of bitterness underneath.

MONKEY   The Man's pet. Smelly and a bit mangy.

SCARY CLOWNS

VAMPIRES

JAZ'S DEAD MUM

A NIGHTWATCHMAN

Scary Play

Scene 1: Kal's Bedroom

*Night-time. It's **Kal**'s 10th birthday sleepover. **Kal**, **Mal**, **Boff**, **Ro**, **Tilly** and **Jaz** sit in a semicircle facing the audience. **Boff**, **Ro**, **Tilly** and **Jaz** are wearing pyjamas or nighties, as would befit each of their characters. **Kal** and **Mal** are wearing the kit of their favourite football team. The light's out but they each have a torch switched on. The beams flash about the room.*

KAL	Ssh!
MAL	Shush!
JAZ	Shut up.
MAL	You shut up!
RO	He's trying to start his story.
JAZ	*I'm* not stopping him.
BOFF	For goodness sake.
MAL	(*mimicking **Boff***) 'For goodness sake'.
KAL	D'you wanna hear it or what?
JAZ/TILLY/RO	Yes!!
MAL	(*louder*) Shut your faces then!!
KAL	(*whispering, angry*) Mal! You'll wake me Dad up.
MAL	Sorry. Sorry Kal. Go on. Go on.

KAL	OK. Torches.

They all shine a beam of torch light up into their faces from under their chins in order to look scary.

KAL	Right. It's about the house on Beech Street.
TILLY	Which house?
MAL	Shush
JAZ	She's just asking!
KAL	The only one still standing on Beech Street. Next to the old car park.
TILLY	Oh I know.
KAL	The only one still standing. Nothing near it but empty space. My Dad says they knocked the rest of 'em down years ago, but the old lady who lived there, she wouldn't move. She wouldn't move. And she had a son who had something wrong with him.

Beat.

TILLY	What was wrong with him?
KAL	He wasn't a kid, he was a grown up, a fully grown man. But he never went out. He didn't have a job or nothing. He wasn't *allowed* out, he was too dangerous. And he had a monkey. A pet monkey.
BOFF	Tut. Nobody has pet monkeys!
KAL	They did in them days. Or he did anyway. I told you, he was different.
JAZ	Did he have Special Needs or something?

KAL	*(impatient)* I dunno, but *anyway* …
TILLY	*(teasing)* Like you Mal …
MAL	*(proudly)* It's Behavioural Difficulties what I've got.
KAL	D'you wanna hear this or what?
MAL	Sorry.
KAL	So they lived there, for years and years, and nobody ever saw them.
JAZ	Nobody ever saw them?
KAL	Nobody.
RO	Didn't they ever go out?
KAL	*They* never went out and nobody ever went in.
BOFF	How did they eat?
KAL	They had their food delivered. The delivery man, he put the food down in a box on their doorstep and nobody ever saw them take it indoors. But ten minutes later, it was always gone.

Beat.

MAL	Someone probably robbed it.
JAZ	Yeah, your brother.
MAL	Yeah, your sister.
JAZ	Yeah, your mother.
MAL	Yeah, your gran.
JAZ	*(with actions)* Your Mum Works in McDonalds Mally.
MAL	*(with actions)* Your Mother's a Minger, Jaz.

8

BOFF	*(to Kal)* How d'you know they were still in there? If no one ever saw them. They might have just moved out.
KAL	I'll tell you how if you'll listen Boff.
BOFF	Go on then. It's not me that's interrupting.
KAL	Because every night the light in the son's bedroom came on at 12 midnight, and every night it went off again at 1am exactly.
TILLY	*(gasps)* That's the Witching Hour.
KAL	That's right.

Beat.

BOFF	How d'you know it was the son's bedroom?
KAL	You could see his shadow, him and his monkey, you could see their shapes against the curtains. Moving about, strange, weird movements. As if they were *doing* something.
JAZ	Doing what?
KAL	Nobody knows. But whatever it was, it was Evil.

Beat. **Kal** *Pauses.*

RO	So what happened?
KAL	D'you wanna know?
RO	Course we wanna know.
KAL	D'you really wanna know? It's not very nice.
TILLY	*(scared)* Ain't it?
KAL	You might be scared.

MAL	We're not scared!
RO	I'm not scared!
KAL	Not you. The girls. And Boff.
JAZ	I'm not scared!
BOFF	It's not true anyway. It's just one of your stories.
KAL	You think so?
BOFF	*(unsure)* Isn't it?
KAL	My Dad says it's true.
BOFF	But …
KAL	You calling my Dad a liar?
BOFF	Nobody would call *your* Dad a liar..
KAL	Shut up then.
JAZ	Go on Kal. What happened?
KAL	He killed her.

Tilly gasps.

JAZ	Who did?
KAL	The son. He killed the old lady.
MAL	*(pleased)* Did he? Was there loads of blood?
KAL	He used a knife, just like this one.

Kal takes a knife that he's been sitting on and brandishes it at everyone. It's an old fashioned knife with an ornate handle and a long blade.

TILLY	*(yelps)* I'm scared.

KAL	My old Granddad's knife.
BOFF	You're not meant to have that knife! Your Dad'll go mad.
KAL	Shut up Boff. My Dad says they carried the old lady out in a black oak coffin, and they walked her son out in a straitjacket.

Beat.

MAL	What's a straitjacket?
BOFF	Oh For Goodness Sake!
RO	What happened to the monkey Kal?
KAL	Good question Ro.

*Silence. **Kal** does another pause. He plays with the knife.*

MAL	So, what *happened* to the bloody monkey?!!
KAL	Will you shush!
MAL	*(quietly)* What happened to it?
KAL	No one knows. But when me Mum and Dad were our age, kids round here used to dare each other to sneak into the house.
RO	Did they?
KAL	Yeah. And one night me Dad and his mate snook in there.
MAL	What was it like?
KAL	It was all sort of, broken up inside. The floorboards were rotting, the wallpaper was peeling, there was a terrible smell, blood stains on the walls and the furniture was falling to pieces.

TILLY	I don't like this.
KAL	And upstairs, in the son's bedroom, lying on his dirty old bed …

Kal does another pause.

TILLY	What? What was there?
KAL	Right there in the middle of the rotten, stinking old bed … *(pause)* … there was a dead monkey, with a knife in its heart.

*As he says the above, **Kal** stabs the knife down as if stabbing the monkey. **Tilly** gasps. Suddenly, the door swings open with a bang. **Kal** drops the knife. Everybody jumps, gasps, screeches.*

KAL	Who's that?

No answer.

KAL	Who is it?
LOU	*(putting on a scary voice)* It's me, the ghost of the monkey, come back to haunt you.

***Tilly** screams.*

KAL	Tilly shut up, it's not the monkey.

*** Kal** makes a dash for the lights and switches them on. Standing in the doorway is **Lou**, wearing boy's pyjamas and cuddling a fluffy old soft toy doggy (Richard). She looks very cute. Standing behind her is **Kal**, his hand on the light switch.*

LOU	Oh. Hello Everybody!

*She does a sheepish little wave. **Kal** grabs her arm suddenly and pulls it behind her back. Threatening to break it.*

12

Lou	Ow!
Kal	I warned you if you came in here during my sleepover I'd break your arm.
Lou	But I can't sleep! You're all talking!
Kal	I warned you. Now I'm going to break your arm.

*He bends **Lou**'s arm right back to near breaking point. **Lou** wails. **Jaz** and **Boff** run to her aid.*

Jaz	Don't do that!
Boff	Kal, she's your sister!
Lou	*(wailing)* I'll tell Daddy!

*Kal drops **Lou**. She falls to the floor whimpering, rubbing her arm, laying it on a bit thick. **Jaz** and **Boff** tend to her.*

Kal	I'm only letting you off because I don't want you to wake anyone up with your fake crying. Little Baby.
Boff	Calm down Kal!
Kal	Shut your mouth Boff, you haven't got a sister, you don't know what I have to go through.
Lou	*(playing up to **Boff** and **Jaz**)* He's always beating me up.
Kal	And you're always lying, now go back to bed. It's my birthday, not yours.

*Beat. **Lou** looks sad.*

Lou	But …

KAL	I'm ten, you're eight. You're a baby. Now get lost.
LOU	I …
KAL	Now! Or I'll tell everyone that thing.
LOU	What thing?
KAL	The thing you're scared of.
LOU	*(beat)* I hate you.

Lou gets up slowly and slopes offstage sadly. She leaves the door open.

KAL	And close the door.

She comes back and closes the door, gently and sadly. Jaz smiles at her. She smiles sadly back. She goes. Almost immediately she comes back and sits on the other side of the door and eavesdrops.

KAL	Little cow.
TILLY	My sister's like that, always butting in.
MAL	*(proudly)* That's what my big brother says about me! And me big sister.
KAL	She thinks she's old enough to do what we do but she's not.
MAL	Yeah!
KAL	She nicks my things, she winds me up *on purpose*, she's always following me around everywhere and if I *do* anything about it she tells on me and I get in trouble with Dad!
JAZ	I think she's cute.
BOFF	So do I.

14

KAL	Shut up Boff.
MAL	Yeah, shut up.

*Awkward pause. **Kal** sulks, **Mal** puts his arm round him.*

TILLY	What we gonna do now then?

__Kal__ shrugs, still sulking.

RO	Any sweets left?
MAL	We've eaten them all.
BOFF	*You've* eaten them all you mean.
MAL	I only had four packets, Tilly had more than me.
TILLY	*(proudly)* I had six!
BOFF	You're gonna lose all your teeth.
MAL	*(mimicking)* 'You're gonna lose all your teeth'.
RO	Shall we have another round of Spin the Bottle?
JAZ	Not *again*.
RO	Why not?
JAZ	You've already snogged Tilly five times Ro.
MAL	Tilly and Ro, Sitting in a tree, Ro stood up and had a wee.

*__Tilly__ giggles, **Ro** smirks and kicks **Mal**.*

BOFF	Maybe, actually, it's time we went to sleep.

They all look at him aghast.

Boff	*(petering out)* If we can't, you know, think of anything else to do. It is late.
Mal	What? No way! It's not even midnight! Let's have another go on Fifa Street Kal.

Tilly and *Jaz* groan.

Tilly	Not again!
Boff	This sleepover's getting really lame.

Kal looks vexed.

Kal	Least I'm *allowed* a sleepover.
Ro	How about some more stories Kal? Tell us another story.
Tilly	Yeah Kal, tell us another story, you're really good at stories.
Jaz	Yeah, go on Kal.
Kal	I'm not going to tell you another story.
Ro	Aw!
Kal	But I have got an idea.
Mal	Fabaluccio!
Boff	Fabaluccio?
Mal	Yeah, it's Italian for Fab.
Boff	Fab what?
Mal	You know, Fab er Tastic?
Boff	It's Fabulous you idiot.
Kal	Do you want to know what my idea is or what?

16

Ro	Yeah.
Tilly	Yeah tell us Kal.
Mal	Yeah man.
Kal	I think we should sneak into the old house on Beech Street.

Silence.

Boff	You've got to be kidding.
Kal	Why not? You scared Boff?
Boff	No, I'm not scared, I'm worried. It's a stupid and dangerous idea.
Mal	*(excited)* I think it's a Fabaluccio idea.
Kal	Ro?
Ro	Er yeah. Great. Let's do it.
Kal	Girls?
Tilly	I'm too scared Kally.
Ro	*(manly)* I'll look after you.
Tilly	*(girly)* Aw! Thank you.
Jaz	I'm not scared. I think it'll be brilliant. Who knows what we'll find in there.
Boff	A health and safety nightmare that's what. The floorboards were rotting even in your Dad's time, one of us is gonna put our foot right through and fall and break our legs.
Kal	You can stay here if you're worried Boff. *(he goes to the door, puts his hand on the handle. **Lou** jumps and runs offstage)* Or is it too *lame* for you?

BOFF	That's not…
KAL	*(cutting in, with actions)* Loser, Loser, Double Loser, take a Picture, look at the Minger.
BOFF	Shut up!
BOFF	Anyone who's got the guts to do it, follow me.

Kal goes out, leaving the door open. Mal follows immediately. Ro takes Tilly's hand.

TILLY	Shall we go?
RO	Well… I suppose so. If Kal says.

They exit, Jaz goes to follow.

BOFF	You're all mad.
JAZ	Why don't you come? You don't have to actually go in there. You could be, like, lookout.
BOFF	I … Dunno.
JAZ	It's either that or face Kal's Dad if he finds us gone.

Jaz exits. Boff hesitates a moment and then follows. After a few seconds Lou comes back onstage. She is now wearing the same full football kit as a her brother and Mal, possibly the previous season's version, handed down from Kal. She's carrying a Batman backpack. She also has a climbing rope over her shoulder, a Winnie the Pooh torch, a compass on a string around her neck, a map book tucked under her arm along with her doggy (Richard) and balaclava rolled up on her head. She looks around, sees the knife that Kal had left lying on the floor. She takes it and puts everything in the Batman backpack. She rolls the balaclava down, switches Kal's light off and switches her torch on. She follows the others, sidling along the wall, as if she's on a special mission for MI5. End of scene.

Scene 2: Bushes outside the haunted house

*We see the house looming large in the background, it looks very rundown and scary. The front door and front upstairs window are visible. **Kal**, **Mal**, **Ro**, **Tilly**, **Jaz** and **Boff** are crouched behind the bushes. They have coats on over their nightwear and are wearing shoes. **Kal**, **Boff** and **Ro** have torches. **Kal** is carrying an axe. Pause. They watch the house.*

TILLY	*(nervous)* It looks very dark.
KAL	*(irritable)* That's why we've got torches.
RO	The front door's all locked up. How we gonna get in?
KAL	That's why we've brought the axe!
BOFF	You're not going to chop it down!
KAL	Why not?
BOFF	Someone'll hear. The police will come. We'll be in trouble!
KAL	We're nowhere near any other houses. How's anyone gonna hear?
MAL	Can I do the chopping Kal?
KAL	We'll take it in turns.
MAL	Fabaluccio! Can I go first?
JAZ	Can I go second?
BOFF	If we get caught, what's your Dad gonna do?
KAL	Skin us alive. That's why we won't be getting caught. *(to **Mal** and **Jaz**)* Come on you two, we'll chop the door down. You lot stay here, we'll give yous a shout when we're ready.

*Mal, **Kal** and **Jaz** go to move off.*

BOFF　　　　　*(trying to stop them)* If this was a scary film you'd
　　　　　　　　be screaming at the screen, 'Don't go in, don't
　　　　　　　　go in!'

KAL　　　　　Oh yeah? When have you seen any scary films.
　　　　　　　　Your Mum won't even let you watch a PG.
　　　　　　　　Your favourite film's *The Wizard of Oz*! *(sarcastic)*
　　　　　　　　Lions and Tigers and Bears, Oh My!

BOFF　　　　　*(it is)* No it's not. And I have seen scary films.
　　　　　　　　And this is what always happens. *Stupid* people
　　　　　　　　go into dangerous and frightening places even
　　　　　　　　though it's completely clear to everyone else in
　　　　　　　　the world that they *shouldn't*.

KAL　　　　　You're bricking it ain't you Boff?

BOFF　　　　　Yeah. I'm bricking it. Anyone in their right
　　　　　　　　mind *would* be bricking it.

KAL　　　　　Loser.

MAL　　　　　I've seen loads of scary films. Me brother gets
　　　　　　　　them out when he's babysitting. You name it,
　　　　　　　　I've seen it. And *I* always scream at the screen
　　　　　　　　'*Do* go in, *do* go in!' cos if they didn't go in there
　　　　　　　　wouldn't *be* a film would there?

*Beat. **Kal** is pleased.*

KAL　　　　　That's right Mally! Put it there son. *(he 'high
　　　　　　　　fives' with **Mal**, or does a special handshake)* Let's
　　　　　　　　go. (**Jaz**, **Mal** and **Kal** go to the house. **Kal** throws
　　　　　　　　Boff a triumphant glance as they go. **Kal**, **Mal** and
　　　　　　　　Jaz reach the front door. **Kal** gets his axe and gives it
　　　　　　　　to **Mal**) There you go Mal. Give it a big swing.

Mal lifts the axe up behind his head and swings down hard on the door.

As he does so, the door swings open with a creak. **Mal** *stumbles forwards.*

MAL   Uh?

Pause.

JAZ   Who did that?

KAL   No one. The door's probably just loose or
               something.

JAZ   You think so?

KAL   Yeah.

Pause. They look at the open door.

JAZ   *(a challenge)* Right. Better go in then Kally.
               Check if it's safe.

Beat. **Kal**, *equal to the challenge, takes a step forwards. He peers inside
the door. He comes out again.*

KAL   *(cocky)* Look's fine to me.

Kal *goes in.* **Mal** *scoots after him, leaving the axe behind.* **Jaz** *hesitates a
moment then goes in. The door creaks closed behind them with a bang.*

TILLY   *(gasps, jumps)* They've gone in! I thought they
               were going to call us!

RO   They were.

TILLY   The door looked like it opened by itself. Did it
               look like it opened by itself to you?

RO   *(scared)* Yeah.

A light in the upstairs window suddenly comes on. They all freeze. **Tilly** *gasps.*

Tilly	*(whispers)* What time is it?
Ro	It's midnight!
Tilly	Oh my Gosh! *(a shadow passes over the window)* Oh My Gosh! It's him!
Ro	*(Scared. Puts his arm around* **Tilly***)* Don't be scared.
Tilly	He's going to kill them!
Boff	Tilly calm down. It's probably torch light. From Kal and them.
Tilly	What about the shadow?!
Boff	It's probably them, isn't it Ro?
Ro	*(unconvincing)* Er, yeah. It's probably them.

Pause, the light in the window goes out.

Tilly	What are we gonna do?
Boff	You can do what you like. I'm staying here. I'm keeping watch.

Ro *and* **Tilly** *look at each other.*

Tilly	Jaz is in there.
Ro	She'll be alright, she's with Kal.
Tilly	But Kal's on one of his *things* isn't he?
Ro	What things?

TILLY	You know, when he gets an idea in his head and he won't back down. And Mal, he just does what Kal wants him to do. They'll end up doing something stupid.
BOFF	Exactly.
TILLY	We'll have to go after them.
RO	*(gulping)* Will we?
TILLY	Yeah. I can't go in there by myself can I Ro?
RO	No.
TILLY	You said you'd look after me.
RO	Yeah. *(regretfully)* I did didn't I.
TILLY	I know you can do it babe. There's more to you than hair gel ain't there?
RO	Er. *(doubtful)* Probably.
TILLY	*(getting up)* Come on. *(she holds her hand out to Ro. He takes it and they go towards the house, hand in hand. As they reach it the door swings open again. Tilly and Ro freeze for a second, then Tilly turns to Boff)* If you never see us again, tell me sister she can have me yellow poncho*, OK?
BOFF	OK. *(Tilly and Ro go in. The door creaks shut behind them. Boff paces by the bushes, looking scared. After a moment he hears a noise – a rustle, then something dropping. Boff jumps. Beat)* Hello? Hello? Is someone there?

No answer. Lights fade. End of scene.

---

* Or other currently desirable girly fashion item.

Scene 3: Inside the house

A dark ramshackle old house. Wallpaper peeling, floorboards broken.

*We are in the downstairs hall. A very precarious looking staircase leads upstairs. If possible, rats scuttle across the floor. **Ro** and **Tilly** enter, shining their torches around.*

Tilly	*(calling)* Jaz!
Ro	Kal! Kally!

The childrens' names echo as they call. No answer. They come to a halt in front of the staircase.

Tilly	They're not down here.
Ro	They must've gone … upstairs.

He shines his torch up the creepy staircase. They both look at it.

Tilly	We'll have to go up.
Ro	I thought you might say that.
Tilly	I wish we hadn't come here.
Ro	So do I.
Tilly	Why do we always do what Kally says?
Ro	He has good ideas. Usually.
Tilly	*This* wasn't a good idea though was it?
Ro	No.

Pause. They look at the staircase.

TILLY	Jaz says we don't have to do what Kal says all the time. She reckons Kal's just a blagger.
RO	That's cos he said no when she asked him to go out with her in Year 4.
TILLY	*(sighs)* No it ain't! She never asked him to … [go out with her!]
RO	She definitely liked him.
TILLY	He's *lying*. She doesn't like Kal, she likes Boff.

Beat. **Tilly** claps her hand over her mouth.

RO	She likes *Boff*!
TILLY	Please don't tell him Ro!
RO	She can't like Boff, he's gay.
TILLY	He's not gay.
RO	He is. He likes books and that don't he? He can't play football. He hasn't even got any trainers!
TILLY	There's nothing wrong with books. Kal likes books.
RO	Yeah but Kal likes football too. *And* he's got a Nintendo DS*.
TILLY	So how comes Kal's mates with Boff then, if Boff's so gay?
RO	Cos Kal's Mum makes him be doesn't she? Cos she's mates with Boff's Mum.
TILLY	Well I like Boff. He's nice. And so does Jaz.

*Nintendo DS or other current equivalent technological wonder.

Ro	I can't believe Jaz fancies Boff.
Tilly	You can talk to Boff. He doesn't take the mickey all the time.
Ro	I don't take the mickey all the time.
Tilly	(*linking **Ro***'*s arm*) Yeah. Jaz reckons I only like you because you're good looking and you wear nice clean fashionable clothes. But I think you've got quite a good personality too.

Ro looks embarrassed. Suddenly there's a noise. An eerie, echoey sound. They jump and cling to each other.

Ro	What was that?
Tilly	I dunno!

The noise comes again. They cling to each other.

Ro	(*panicking*) Do we have to go up them stairs?
Tilly	(*trying not to panic*) Whenever I'm scared my Dad always says to me, imagine you're Invincible.
Ro	Invisible?
Tilly	Invincible. Like, no one can beat you.
Ro	Like Batman or something?
Tilly	Yeah, like Batman or Superman or something like that.
Ro	I've never been any good at nothing like that.
Tilly	Like what?
Ro	Like being Invincible. Kally and Mal always look after me.

TILLY	Yeah. Same with me and Jaz. But we got to help *them* this time innit?
RO	I'm scared Tilly.
TILLY	So am I. But we gotta show 'em *we* can be brave too. Yeah?

Beat.

RO	Yeah. We gotta show 'em. *(they look up the staircase. The echoey noise is heard again. **Ro** starts crying)* I wish we could just go home.
TILLY	*(also crying)* Yeah. So do I.

Lights fade. End of scene.

Scene 4: Outside the house

Boff is still standing next to the bushes looking nervous. He hears another noise. He jumps.

Boff   Look! Whoever you are, you better show yourself! I've got a mobile in my anorak pocket. I will call the police!

*There is a lot of activity in the bushes as someone tries to extricate themselves. After a bit, **Lou** emerges. She's all togged up and carrying her equipment.*

Lou   I thought your Mum said you weren't allowed to have a mobile.

Boff   What are *you* doing here?!!

Lou   *I* want to sneak in the house too!

Boff   What? You're as crazy as your brother.

Lou   My brother's not crazy. Don't *say* that about him!

*She goes to thump **Boff**. He steps out of the way.*

Boff   I don't understand you. Why do you always stick up for him? He's horrible to you.

Lou   He's not.

Boff   He *is* Lou. He nearly broke your arm before.

Lou   He didn't. It looked worse than it was.

She rubs her arm.

Boff   He treats you really badly. He won't let you join in anything, he makes fun of you, he beats you up.

LOU	He loves me very much. Brothers and sisters always fight a lot. That's what my mum says. It's called sidling ribaldry.
BOFF	Go home and go to bed Lou.
LOU	*(showing her stuffed doggie)* He bought me Richard, that's how much he loves me. For Christmas when I was a baby. The best dog in the world.

She hugs Richard.

BOFF	Look. You don't want Richard to get hurt do you?
LOU	No.
BOFF	Then go home and tell your Dad what's happened. Someone needs to do something to stop all this ... craziness.
LOU	Tell my Dad? That *would* be crazy. Have they gone in already?
BOFF	Yes. I mean no.
LOU	What?
BOFF	No. They haven't. They've all, er, gone to look round the back. The front door's all locked up. We probably can't get in.
LOU	I've got a rope! We can climb up to a window and pull each other up!
BOFF	Don't be silly. I'd go home if I was you, before Kal catches you.
LOU	No.
BOFF	He'll tell everyone that thing you're scared of.

A torch light shines in the upstairs window. They both see it.

Lou   What's that light?

Boff   What light?

The light shines again.

Lou   That light.

Boff   Er …

Lou   I thought you said they hadn't gone in? *(Beat. The door swings open with a creak. Pause. **Lou** looks at **Boff**)* I thought you said the door was locked?

Boff   Please don't go in there Lou.

Lou   You come in too if you're worried about me.

Boff   I'm, er, on 'Look Out'.

Lou   Look out for what? The scary stuff's in there isn't it? Not out here.

Boff   No but … there might be police coming. Or something. Or your Dad! So I need to … look out.

Lou   You're going to let me go in by myself aren't you? *(pause. **Boff** looks away. **Lou** shakes her head sadly)*

                   See ya Boff.

***Lou** goes into the house, possibly sidling like a spy along the wall on the way in. She picks up the axe left earlier by **Mal**. The door swings shut behind her.*

Boff   Why won't anyone listen to me!

Scene 5: Inside the house

*Upstairs landing. **Ro** and **Tilly** enter, clinging to each other. There's a room to the side of the stairs with the door closed. They shine their torches on it and go towards it.*

TILLY	Jaz! Mal!
RO	Kal!

They stop outside the door.

TILLY	They're not in the bathroom.
RO	They're not in the boxroom.
TILLY	They're not in the cupboard.
RO	They're not downstairs.

They stop outside the door.

TILLY	This is the only room left.
RO	The front bedroom.
TILLY	His room.
RO	Yeah.

*Pause. During the following **The Man** comes quietly onstage. He is very neatly dressed in a plain suit. He walks silently and slowly across the landing until he is standing behind **Ro** and **Tilly**. He has **the monkey** with him, on a lead. **Tilly** and **Ro** don't see him.*

TILLY	*(whispers)* What if they're dead?
RO	Don't say that.

TILLY	We've been calling them and calling them. Why haven't they answered?
RO	Maybe they've gone back outside.
TILLY	I hope so.
RO	Why don't we just go?
TILLY	We've got to look in there first. What if they're in there and they need our help? We'd never forgive ourselves.
RO	I've got a very bad feeling about that room.
TILLY	I thought you wanted to show 'em how brave you can be.

Beat.

RO	*(gulping)* Right. We'll just open the door quickly. Look in, quickly like. Then go home.
TILLY	*(nervous)* OK.

Tilly and Ro hold hands. They take a step towards the door. Ro puts his hand on the handle.

THE MAN	*(calmly)* I wouldn't go in there if I was you.

*Tilly and Ro jump and screech. They turn around to see **The Man**. Silence for a moment. He looks at them. **The monkey** sniffs them.*

TILLY	*(terrified)* Who are you?
THE MAN	Who do you think I am?
TILLY	I don't know. Where's our friends?
THE MAN	Your friends?

32

Ro	Are … you … him?
The Man	Him?
Tilly	Is this your house? Our friends came in here. They didn't mean to trespass or nothing. It was just for fun.
The Man	Ah. Fun. I see.
Ro	*(trembling)* They didn't mean any harm. Please let them out. We all just want to go home. Don't we Tilly?
The Man	You think I've got your friends in that room?

Beat.

Ro	Yes.
Tilly	No!
Tilly	*(squeezing **Ro**'s hand)* No. Course not. *Is* this your house?
The Man	This house is dangerous. But if you come with me and do as you're told, I'll make it safe.
Tilly	Thank you. But I think we're gonna go now, eh Ro?
Ro	Er yeah. We're gonna go.

*Ro and **Tilly** start edging towards the stairs. **The Man** watches them for a moment.*

The Man	Don't you want to know about my monkey?
Ro	No, we'd better be …

Suddenly there is a call from inside the room. It sounds like Jaz.

JAZ   *(offstage)* Tilly!

*Tilly's name echoes loudly. **Ro** and **Tilly** stop.*

TILLY   What was that?

THE MAN   I didn't hear anything.

TILLY   I thought I heard my best mate. Jaz.

THE MAN   Stay here and talk to me. I *might* have seen her.

RO   Tilly let's go.

*Beat. **Tilly** takes a few steps back up. She swallows.*

TILLY   What did you say your monkey was called?

THE MAN   S/He's called Monkey. Do you want to stroke
                 him/her?

TILLY   Yes.

*Tilly goes to **the monkey**. She stretches her hand out to pet him/her.
Suddenly **the monkey** grabs her. **Tilly** struggles but **the monkey** holds
her tight, covers her mouth.*

THE MAN   Don't be frightened. If you do as I say, all will
                 be well. *(he opens the door to the bedroom. We can't
                 see inside. To **Ro**)* You'd better come too.
                 Monkey gets a bit over enthusiastic sometimes.
                 Your friend might need your help.

*Monkey pushes **Tilly** hard into the room. **Ro**, sobbing and shaking,
follows. **The Man** lets them through the door, then slips in himself. The
door closes quietly behind them.*

34

Scene 6: Outside the house

*Boff, looking towards the house. He wants to go in after **Lou** but he's really scared, and upset with himself for being scared.*

BOFF   *(trying to convince himself)* I *can* be brave, I *can* be brave, I *can* be brave, I *can. (pause. He looks at the house)* Oh Mummy.

He paces a bit, takes a few steps towards the house, hears a noise, runs back again. He starts to recite 'Lions and Tigers and Bears, Oh My' from The Wizard of Oz. *He builds up his confidence and starts to recite louder and faster as the song goes on. He is just about to march confidently into the house when the light in the upstairs window comes on full blast and a small crashing sound is heard. He stops in his tracks, stares in horror at the window, then turns on his heels and runs offstage.*

Scene 7: The bedroom/the landing

*Lights up on **Kal**, **Mal**, **Jaz**, **Tilly** and **Ro** tied up and sitting on and around a stained old bed in the middle of the bedroom. There are strange drawings and paintings on the walls of the room. We can still see the landing at the other side of the bedroom door. There is a broken glass on the floor. **The Man** stands watching the children. **The monkey** sweeps up the glass with a dust pan and brush.*

THE MAN	Thank you Monkey. Clumsy boy Ro!
TILLY	*(to **Jaz**)* What's going on?
JAZ	I dunno.
KAL	He's mad, that's what's going on. My Dad's gonna kill you if you do anything to us.
THE MAN	Who said *I'm* going to do anything? We were having an interesting talk before your friends decided to join us.
KAL	I don't think it was interesting.
THE MAN	About *fear* wasn't it?
KAL	You're weird and sick.
THE MAN	What's your biggest fear Kal? Come on.
KAL	I don't have no biggest fears.
THE MAN	Come on. I'll let you go if you tell me.

Beat.

RO	*(scared, to **Jaz**)* Does he mean he'll let us go if we tell him what we're scared of?
KAL	Don't tell him anything Ro.

THE MAN	Don't listen to Kal Ro, what does Kal know? It was, after all, Kal's idea to come *here. (beat)* So. Who wants to leave?
JAZ	Why tie us up like this? You could've asked us what we were scared of when we first came in.
THE MAN	You were trespassing on my property. Isn't a man allowed to make his own house safe from intruders?
KAL	We're ten years old, we're not very big intruders.
THE MAN	*(snapping nastily)* Children can be *very* bad. Don't you watch television?

Pause.

JAZ	Nobody has lived in this house for years. How come it's your property?
THE MAN	That's true. No one has lived here. But there has always been an owner, and now the owner's back.

Beat.

TILLY	*Are* you the owner then?
THE MAN	Yes.
KAL	So where've you been?
THE MAN	Let's just say, I've been away.
KAL	Why do you want to know what we're scared of?
THE MAN	It's a … project I'm working on.

MAL	I'm doing a Project at school! It's about Queen Victoria.
KAL	Shut up Mal.
MAL	Sorry.
THE MAN	So don't *any* of you want to leave?
MAL	I do!
KAL	Mal, shut up.
MAL	But ...
KAL	*(to **Man**)* What are *you* scared of?

Beat.

THE MAN	Mm. Interesting question.
KAL	I bet you won't tell us.
THE MAN	I could say Ghosts. Or Witches. Or Monsters or Banshees or Spectres or Demons.

Beat.

JAZ	So? Which one is it?
THE MAN	None of them. Not really. People aren't really frightened of things like that because things like that don't really exist do they? They're just stories. They're just figments of the imagination.
MAL	I've got a Figment in my Imagination! My Mum says that when I've been lying about something.
THE MAN	Kal's got a good imagination, haven't you Kal? Good at stories aren't you? Good at telling lies.

KAL	Shut up freak.
THE MAN	But lies aren't real. And people are *really* scared of real things. Things that could really happen to them. Plane crashes, diseases, earthquakes, hurricanes, guns, bombs.
KAL	*(to **Monkey**)* Knives?

Monkey flinches a little.

MAL	I ain't scared of plane crashes and that.
THE MAN	Aren't you Mal?
MAL	It's really funny what I'm scared of.
KAL	Mal.
MAL	It's stupid really. Cos really, they're meant to make you laugh not scare you. But it's their faces, the make-up. It doesn't look funny to me. It looks horrible.
JAZ	Mal!
THE MAN	*(playful)* Ah! I think I can guess what you're talking about Mally.
MAL	*(pleased)* Go on then! I bet you can't!
KAL	Mal will you … *[shut up]*
THE MAN	*(cutting in)* Is it … something to do with the circus?
MAL	*(amazed)* Yeah!
KAL	Mal, shut up!
THE MAN	It's clowns isn't it?

MAL	Yeah, man! How did you guess that?!
JAZ	Mal you idiot!
MAL	What?
JAZ	You've told him!
MAL	Oh.
THE MAN	Don't worry Mal. That's fine. You've told me. You can go.

*Monkey unties **Mal**. Beat.*

THE MAN	Off you go.
MAL	Fabaluccio! Look, he's letting me go. You just have to tell him. (***The Man*** *opens the door for **Mal**. **Mal*** *gets up and goes out*) See you soon guys. (***Mal*** *goes through the door. **The Man*** *closes it behind him. He stays facing the door, as if he can see through it. On the landing, weird, distorted circus/fairground music starts playing. A sign on the wall lights up: The House of Fun*) What's this?
ECHOEY VOICE	*(offstage)* Welcome to the House of Fun Malcolm.

*Cackling, distorted laughter starts echoing round the landing. Harsh and nasty. An enormous clown comes bouncing onto the stage. He has really horrible make-up on, a grimacing red smile, and a big garish clown suit. **Mal** screams. The clown envelops him inside his suit in a big suffocating embrace. Other clowns follow, bouncing all over the stage, cackling maniacally. **Mal** screams and struggles but he can't get free. They carry him away. During this, **The Man** faces the door from the other side and watches. He enjoys **Mal**'s fear. It's as if it's been giving him nourishment. Once **Mal** has been carried off, he turns back to the room.*

THE MAN	There you are, simple as that. Tell me what you're scared of and I'll let you go.

Beat.

Ro	I'll tell you.
Kal	Ro!
Ro	*(scared)* I want to get out of here Kal. We can all get out like Mal if we just tell him.
Kal	No way. I'm not gonna tell him anything. Don't tell him! He's up to something!
Ro	You're not the boss Kal. We don't have to do what *you* say all the time. *(to **the monkey** and* **The Man***)* You can untie me.

The Man *gestures to* **Monkey**. **Monkey** *unties* **Ro**.

Kal	Ro!
Ro	I just have to tell you then I can go?
The Man	Yes.
Ro	It's Vampires.
The Man	Vampires. I see. What is it about them?
Ro	*(duh)* They sink their teeth into your neck and suck out all your blood?
The Man	And how would that feel?
Ro	It'd … it'd feel like … like fainting, like going dizzy and sick and falling and banging your head on the ground. And your neck, them big teeth in your neck, that'd hurt man. That'd really hurt. And it'd be really messy too. The blood'd get all over your nice clean clothes and mess 'em up. That'd be terrible.

Beat.

THE MAN   Thank you. You may go.

The Man goes to the door and opens it for Ro.

RO   See! Don't listen to Kal. We just have to tell
                 him! Just tell the guy what you're scared of
                 Tilly. I'll see you outside.

*Ro goes through the door and onto the landing. The Man closes the door
behind him. Standing on the landing is a vampire. It is animalistic and
savage looking.*

RO   Oh.

*Ro turns to run away but too late. The vampire grabs him. Other
vampires come. Ro is paralysed with fear. The vampires crowd round
him in a huddle. They attack his neck violently. The Man watches
'through' the door. At the same time in the bedroom, Kal struggles and
bangs about.*

KAL   He's doing something to them, I know he is! Let
                 us go! Let us go!!

*He bangs against the bed frame, straining to break his ties. The monkey
jumps on Kal, wrestles him to the ground and sits on him. Finally the
vampires carry Ro offstage, bleeding. The Man turns back to the room.
He sees Kal with the monkey restraining him.*

THE MAN   Oh dear. You're being naughty Kal. Now I'm
                 really going to have to dish out some
                 punishment.

Lights go out in the bedroom.

42

Scene 8: The landing

Lou sidles out of the shadows. She has been watching.

Lou   There's definitely something weird going on here.

She sidles along the wall and listens at the bedroom door. She paces as bit. She looks worried/angry/ready for action. She delves into her backpack. She takes out a few things. The compass, the map, and action man magazine, the knife, a poster of McFly*, a toy walkie talkie. Finally she finds a toy spy headset. She puts the other stuff back in, then wraps the headset around her head. It has an X-ray vision eye piece on it. She goes to the door and tries to stare through it with the X-ray eye. It doesn't work, she takes it off and throws it to the ground. She picks up Richard.

Lou   *(to Richard)* Well Richard, it looks like the batteries have run out on the X-Ray Spex Super Vision Eye Piece. Again. We're going to have to try something else. We must be clever, it's our Most Important Mission Ever. Only you and me can rescue these kids from this terrible nightmare.

She reaches back into her backpack again and brings out the axe she picked up earlier. The door creaks. Lou runs back into the shadows. The door opens and Monkey comes out. Monkey runs across the landing and exits. Lou steps out of the shadows and watches him go off through a toy telescope. A few seconds pass. Monkey comes back, dressed in a dentist's coat and mask. He/She is dragging a dentist's chair on wheels which squeak. Lou hides. Monkey goes back to the bedroom, closing the door behind him. Lou steps out of the shadows, runs up to the door and goes to hit it with the axe. The head of the axe falls off. Lou stares at it.

Lou   Mm. I thought Daddy said he was going to fix that.

* Or other current BoyPop band

(to Richard) Right. We'll have to think of something else Richard. But be careful. That monkey looks really strong. *(Richard whispers something in **Lou**'s ear)* What's that? Richard, you're a genius! *(she takes the rope off her shoulder and looks at it)* I think it'll be long enough.

She exits down the stairs, sliding like a spy. End of scene.

Scene 9: The bedroom

*Kal is tied up more firmly to the bed and he has also been gagged. **Tilly** is strapped to the dentist's chair. **The monkey** is standing over her. It has an enormous syringe needle in one hand and a hand powered drill in the other. It is wearing plastic hygiene gloves. **Tilly** is shaking with fear.*

THE MAN	So. Jaz. Tell me what you're scared of. *(nastily)* Or Tilly gets it right in the teeth.
JAZ	You said we could go if we told you our fears!
THE MAN	Yes but then Kal was naughty wasn't he?
JAZ	But Tilly wasn't naughty! Tilly *told* you what she's scared of and now you've done this to her.
THE MAN	Yes, because Kal was naughty. And now we know what scares Tilly. And a very understandable fear it is. I never liked having my teeth drilled either. It's a horrible *noise* isn't it?

*Monkey gives the drill a quick whizz. **Tilly** screams.*

JAZ	But why aren't you punishing Kal, this is all Kal's fault, Kal got us into it in the first place!
THE MAN	Yes. He's been bad. And here you see the consequences of his actions. Too late for Kally. But *you* can be good. You can save Tilly. If you'll only tell me, you and Tilly can walk free.
JAZ	I dunno, I …

*The Man leans over **Tilly** and looks into her mouth.*

THE MAN	Oh dear. I think Tilly's been eating too many sweeties. We're going to have to drill them all out.

Monkey switches the drill on and moves it slowly towards Tilly's mouth.

JAZ   Alright! Alright! I'll tell you.

Monkey switches the drill off.

THE MAN   Good girl. I knew you'd see sense. *(Pause. Jaz struggles with herself)* Come on Jaz. We're all *dying* to hear. Aren't we Monkey?

The Monkey puts its hand by its ear and cranes towards Jaz. Jaz looks down.

JAZ   *(mumbling)* It's to do with my Mum.

THE MAN   Pardon Jasmine? I can't quite hear you.

JAZ   My Mum. I'm frightened of anything happening to her.

THE MAN   *(beat)* Really?

JAZ   Yes. I've been like that since I was little, since my Dad … went away. I don't even like her going out at night. You know, out with her friends for a drink or something. I always think something's going to happen to her.

Beat.

THE MAN   What kind of things?

During the below, The Man seems to puff up and grow taller.

JAZ   *(shrugs)* Could be anything. She could get run over by a car, or fall in front of a train, or get shot by accident in a bank raid. Or she could catch some terrible illness or choke on a fishbone or get bitten by a rabid dog. She could eat something dodgy and get salmonella and get admitted to hospital only to catch a terrible hospital bug. And if she ever manages to recover from that she could catch Legionnaires' Disease from the Jacuzzi down the gym and just die anyway. I get these terrible dreams. My Mum, lying in a coffin, dead. And I'm looking down on her. She looks beautiful. At rest. But suddenly she opens her eyes, she looks at me hard, her hand comes up and she grabs me.

Pause. Everyone is quiet for a moment.

THE MAN   Thank you so much for sharing Jasmine. *(nastily)* Personally, I think a coffin's the best place for a mother.

*Monkey and **The Man** both snigger horribly.*

THE MAN   You can go now Jasmine. Bye bye.

Beat.

JAZ   What about Tilly?

THE MAN   Tilly's coming soon.

*He opens the door. **Jaz** stands up.*

JAZ   *(hesitating)* I dunno.

THE MAN   *(impatient)* Oh do get a move on Jaz.

*He pushes **Jaz** through the door and slams it behind her. A coffin rolls onto the landing with 'R.I.P. Mum' written on it. **Jaz** stares gob-*

*smacked. The coffin lid creaks open and we see **Jaz's Mum** lying inside.*
*Jaz walks towards it like a zombie. She leans over. **Jaz's mum** opens her*
*eyes, grabs **Jaz's** arm and drags her into the coffin. **Jaz** struggles but the*
lid closes on her and the coffin glides back offstage. Simultaneously, in the
*bedroom, **the monkey** leans over **Tilly**, brandishing the drill and*
*syringe. S/he drills viciously at **Tilly's** mouth. **Tilly** tries to scream. There*
*is blood. **Kal** struggles, bangs about, furious. The coffin has now gone off.*
*Finally, **Tilly** lies limp. **Monkey** opens the bedroom door and pushes*
***Tilly** out, chair wheels squeaking. S/he wheels chair across the landing*
and off, then comes back, pulling off his/her plastic gloves. During this
***The Man** watches **Kal**. **Kal** stares back at the man defiantly, struggling.*

THE MAN   Did you want to say something to me Kal?
                 *(**Kal** tries to speak through his gag)* Monkey, I
                 think Kal has a comment he wants to make.

***Monkey** takes **Kal's** gag off.*

KAL   *(angrily)* I know what you're doing you
                 Freak!!!

THE MAN   Oh do you, how interesting. Do tell.

***Monkey** and **The Man** sit down and listen attentively.*

KAL   You're feeding off people's fear aren't you? Like
                 it's food or something. Well I'm not going to
                 give you anything more to eat. Because I'm not
                 scared of anything, OK?! And if I was I
                 wouldn't tell you and you wouldn't be able to
                 do anything about it because no one's left.
                 You've got no one left to threaten me with!

*Just then, the bedroom window flies open and **Lou** jumps in with a*
flourish and a yell, landing on the floor in front of them. There may even
be a crash of breaking glass as she jumps through. She has her balaclava
rolled down. She takes up a martial arts stance and yells out.

LOU	You leave my brother alone!!!

The balaclava muffles her.

THE MAN	Beg Pardon?

She rolls the balaclava up.

LOU	You leave my brother alone!!!!
KAL	Oh for Crying Out Loud Lou!!!
LOU	*(hurt)* What? I'm here to save you!
KAL	You've just ruined everything, you stupid *cow*!
LOU	*(near tears)* But I, I climbed all the way up and everything. I've grazed both my knees. You never want me to join in anything!!!

She starts wailing.

KAL	Shut up! Stop being such a baby! And that's *my* backpack.
LOU	*(shouting)* It *used* to be yours. You gave it to *me* last week!
KAL	Did I?
LOU	Yes. *(beat. **Lou** looks at **The Man**)* Who're you?
THE MAN	I'm your friend Lou.
KAL	Don't listen to him Lou. He's not anybody's friend. And don't, whatever you do, tell him that thing you're scared of.
LOU	I won't. You're the only person in the world that knows that. You and Mum.

KAL   And Dad.

LOU   And Daddy. And Richard. And Suzy next door.
               That's all.

THE MAN   *(delighted)* Ah. A Great Big Secret. How
               Wonderful!

LOU   I'll never tell you. It's very very embarrassing.

THE MAN   If you don't, my Monkey will kill your brother.

LOU   *(beat)* What? (**Monkey** *goes to* **Kal**. *S/he puts
               his/her hands round* **Kal**'s *neck and pushes his head
               back, ready to strangle him*) Kal!

Scene 10: Outside

*Enter **Boff**, creeping back onstage, looking warily towards the upstairs window, which is now open with **Lou***'*s rope dangling down from it. He stops and stares up at the window.*

BOFF   Lou!

Boff** runs to **Lou'*s rope, dangling from the window. He grabs it. He looks up and braces himself for the climb. He tugs on the rope and puts one foot on the wall, ready. The rope falls down and lands in a pile beside him. **Boff** runs to the door and goes to open it. He pulls on the handle. It won't open. He pulls harder. No joy. He rattles and pulls and pulls. It won't open.*

BOFF   *(frustrated)* Aaaaahhhhh!!!! *(He kicks the wall in frustration. A bit too hard. He hurts his foot and hops about)* Owwww!!!!

Scene 11: The bedroom

*Monkey has **Kal** round the neck, strangling him. **Kal** chokes. **Lou** watches in horror.*

LOU	Please. Please! Make it stop!
THE MAN	If you tell me what you're scared of I will.
LOU	OK! I'll tell you! I'll tell you.
KAL	*(in between chokes)* Don't tell him Lou!
THE MAN	I promise not to tell another living soul what it is.
LOU	It's ... it's ...
KAL	No! Stop! Stop! Let her go. *I'll* tell you alright! **(Monkey** *loosens his/her grip on **Kal'**s neck. **Kal** is defeated)* I'll tell you what I'm scared of. Let her go.

The Man claps his hands together.

THE MAN	Oh goody! Got you! I knew I would in the end.
LOU	Kal!

Kal goes quiet. Pause.

THE MAN	*(excited)* Come on then, fire away! *(another pause. **Kal** struggles with himself)* Oh do hurry up Kally, the suspense is killing me.
KAL	It's ... my Dad.
THE MAN	*(beat)* Ah. Like Jaz with her Mum!

KAL	No. Not like Jaz with her Mum! It's him. Himself. I'm frightened of him. I'm frightened of my Dad, OK?!

Beat.

THE MAN	Why?
KAL	Because he's scary! Why d'you think?! I'm not the only one that thinks so. A lot of people are scared of my Dad.
LOU	I'm not.
KAL	No. Cos you're his little Princess aren't you.
LOU	I'm not! I don't even like Princesses.
THE MAN	*(very interested)* Is he … cruel to you?

Monkey whimpers.

KAL	No, not cruel, firm. And a bit shouty sometimes. But he has to be doesn't he? He has to be with me because I'm out of order sometimes and he can't put up with *that* can he?
THE MAN	Does he shut you up in dark cupboards?

Monkey whimpers some more.

KAL	No!
THE MAN	Does he burn you with his cigarette?
KAL	Of course he doesn't! He doesn't even smoke!
THE MAN	Does he make you sit, in a bath of freezing cold water, in the middle of winter, for fifteen long and tortuous hours?

*Monkey holds **The Man's** hand and strokes it comfortingly.*

KAL	No.
THE MAN	Then what's to be scared of?!!

Beat.

KAL	He, well, sometimes I think he … sometimes, when he's cross with me, I think *(mumbles)* he doesn't like me.
THE MAN	Speak up Kal!!!
KAL	He doesn't like me.

Pause. **Kal** *is one the verge of crying.* **Lou** *goes to him and puts her arm around his shoulders.*

LOU	He does like you.
KAL	How do *you* know?
LOU	He says it. He's very proud of you, that's what he says. That time when you got best marks in the Maths test. And when you made that really good Dr. Who Tardis out of egg boxes. I heard him telling Mum.

Beat.

KAL	Well he never said anything to me.
LOU	Maybe he feels embarrassed.
KAL	D'you think so?
LOU	Yeah. Cos men're *like* that aren't they. That's what Mum says anyway.

Beat.

THE MAN	Is that it then?

KAL	(embarrassed) Yes.
THE MAN	(scornful) Your Dad's a bit strict with you? That's it?
KAL	Yes.
THE MAN	(slowly, with actions) Loser Loser, Double Loser, Take a Picture. Look at Minger.
KAL	(upset) Shut up! You ain't even got a Dad!
THE MAN	Oh boo hoo. You've got no idea. (disappointed) Untie him Monkey. I thought it was going to be something good. (**Monkey** unties **Kal**. **The Man** holds the door open) Bye bye, Boring Boy.
KAL	What about Lou?
THE MAN	Lou hasn't told me her secret.

Monkey goes behind Lou and holds her with her arm twisted behind her back.

KAL	If you don't let Lou go then I'm not going either. Don't tell him Lou.
THE MAN	Goodbye Kal.
KAL	I'm not going.
THE MAN	Goodbye!!!

*He starts pushing **Kal** through the door. **Kal** pushes back. They struggle for a moment. **Lou** looks around desperately then sees her Batman backpack.*

LOU	(quickly) It's knives!
KAL	What?
THE MAN	What?

Monkey whimpers.

LOU   That's what I'm scared of. *(hinting to **Kal**)* You know Kal. Granddad's Nasty Scary Old Knife. *(**Monkey** whimpers)* Luckily I haven't seen it for a while.

*She nods towards the backpack. **Kal** twigs, takes a sudden lunge away from **The Man** and grabs the bag. He turns it upside down, all the stuff, including Richard, falls out. **Kal** grabs the knife. **Lou**, meanwhile makes a sudden twist out of the **Monkey**'s grasp. They fight. **Lou** stamps hard on **Monkey**'s foot, **Monkey** whimpers and hops. **Lou** punches **Monkey**. At the same time, **The Man** goes to grab **Kal** but **Kal** slides away. He grabs **Monkey** and holds the knife to his/her heart. **The Man** grabs **Lou**. Stand off.*

KAL   Let my sister go or I'll kill your dirty mangy fleabitten stinking old ape!

Monkey is terrified of the knife. He whimpers and shakes.

THE MAN   *(very worried)* Please. Please. Not the knife!

KAL   That's what *you're* scared of isn't it? Someone sticking a knife in your precious Monkey's heart.

THE MAN   Please.

KAL   He/she's your only friend isn't he/she? A dirty minging animal.

THE MAN   You mustn't hurt him/her.

KAL   Let my sister go. *(**The Man** hesitates for a moment, then lets **Lou** go)* Run Lou!

Lou runs out.

THE MAN   Let go of my Monkey please.

KAL	Bring my friends back first.
THE MAN	Your friends have gone.
KAL	Bring them back or I'll kill it.

*Kal brandishes the knife at **Monkey**'s throat. **Monkey** screeches.*

THE MAN	*(panicking)* Alright, alright. I'll bring them back.

*He clicks his fingers. Music. The children are escorted back onstage by their respective 'fears'. i.e. **Mal** is brought back by a clown, **Ro** by a vampire, **Jaz** by her dead mum, and **Tilly** by a dentist. The fears now seem kind and caring. They deliver the children and then leave. As this all happens, **The Man** seems to become smaller and weaker.*

TILLY	Ro?
JAZ	What happened?
RO	I dunno.
MAL	Where are we? *(**Kal** sees them through the open door)*
KAL	Right.

*He edges to the doorway, still holding **Monkey**. When he gets into the doorway he throws **Monkey** to the floor. **Monkey** weeps. **The Man** goes to him/her. They hug. **The Man** weeps.*

THE MAN	My precious. My angel.

Kal slams the door shut on them.

KAL	*(to the others)* Run!

They all run offstage as quickly as possible. End of scene. Music.

Scene 12: outside the house

Kal and Lou are in the middle of explaining to Boff and the other kids what happened.

KAL   And then the Monkey drilled your teeth out!

TILLY   *(amazed)* What?

MAL   A monkey? Drilling teeth? Fabaluccio!

KAL   You must remember!

BOFF   This is ridiculous. *(to Jaz)* This is just one of his stories.

LOU   It's not! My brother is not a liar!

Beat.

KAL   Thanks Lou.

Kal gives Lou a quick awkward pat on the back. She looks made up.

BOFF   *(to Lou)* You're just sticking up for him again. You know it's not true.

LOU   No I'm not!

JAZ   *(to Kal, cutting in)* You're imagination is really out of control you know Kal. Or is it just an excuse. Because you came screaming out of that room like a little baby!

TILLY   *(cocky)* Yeah, me and Ro didn't find it scary in there at all did we Ro?

RO   *(evasive)* Er no. Not at all.

KAL	Look. I don't care what you think. We need to get away from here.
LOU	Please listen to him!
BOFF	*(sighs)* Just because he brought you Richard doesn't mean you always have to stand by him. *He* probably didn't even buy Richard, it was probably your Mum!

Beat.

LOU	RICHARD!
KAL	Oh For …
LOU	RICHARD!
KAL	We can't go back in there Lou.
LOU	*(wailing)* RICHARD!
KAL	It's just a bit of stuffed fur!
BOFF	That's not a very nice thing to say about Richard!
KAL	What's it got to do with You!!
BOFF	Nothing. I just … I understand about Richard that's all. Cuddlies are very important to people.
KAL	*(beat)* You've got one haven't you.
BOFF	Shut up.
KAL	You have. Boff's got a cuddly!
JAZ	Actually Kal, so have I.
TILLY	And me.
RO	Er yeah. I've got one too.

MAL	I've got a T-Rex!
JAZ	T-Rexes aren't cuddly Mal.
MAL	You're telling me. Those teeth don't half hurt when you lie on them!
BOFF	Richard is more than just a bit of fur.
KAL	*(to Boff)* Alright then. If Richard is so important, you go back in there and get him.

*Beat. **Boff** hovers.*

KAL	Come on Boff. If what I told you ain't true, what's to be scared of? *(**Lou** sobs)* Come on. I've been in, Mal's been in, Jaz's been in there. Even Ro and Tilly.

*Ro and **Tilly** look proudly at each other.*

BOFF	I did try and get in you know.
KAL	*(disbelieving)* Oh yeah?
BOFF	Yes! The door seemed to have locked itself up again, and the rope fell down.
KAL	Yeah right. Chicken boy.
BOFF	I'm not chicken I …
KAL	Little Girl.
BOFF	I *did* try. We don't all tell lies all the time Kal.
KAL	Stop calling me a liar.
BOFF	Well it is all a bit far-fetched. A Monkey dressed as a Dentist!

60

KAL	So go in and get Richard then. Do something brave for once in your life.

*Pause. **Boff** takes a big breath.*

BOFF	Alright. Alright. I'll go.

Boff takes a deep breath and then moves purposefully towards the house. He's about to reach the door when…

KAL	(bit worried) Boff.
BOFF	What?
KAL	Er, take this. In case I'm telling the truth.

*He takes the knife out of his pocket and gives it to **Boff**. **Boff** pockets the knife. The door is already open. They all watch. **Boff** hesitates, turns his torch on, then suddenly runs in, very fast. The door doesn't shut. We hear **Boff** singing 'Lions and Tigers and Bears' inside the house as he runs upstairs. Torch light flashes in the upstairs window. A flurry of shadows is seen. Suddenly, there is a loud scream.*

TILLY	Oh My Gosh!!
JAZ	Boff!
LOU	Richard!

*Jaz and **Kal** run towards the house but **Boff** comes running out, fast as he can, carrying Richard. He has no knife. He runs into **Jaz** and **Kal**. **Jaz** throws her arms around him.*

KAL	What happened?!!
JAZ	Are you alright?

Boff hugs Jaz back for a sec. Then they both realise what they are doing and jump apart. Boff gives Richard to Lou. She cuddles him happily.

Lou	Richard!!
Mal	What happened Boffy?
Boff	*(still scared, out of breath)* I went upstairs.
Mal	Yeah?
Boff	It was really creepy in there. And very dangerous. I'm surprised none of you broke their ankle!
Kal	What did you see?
Boff	I went in the bedroom. It was really dark and quiet.
Kal	And?
Boff	There was a bed.
Tilly	I'm scared.
Boff	And lying on the bed was a stuffed Toy Monkey.

Beat.

Kal	A toy?
Boff	Yeah. And Richard was lying next to him. So I went to grab Richard. And just as I put my hand on him I swear I saw the Monkey move!
Ro	No!
Boff	Yeah! It must have been a trick of the light. But I panicked. I screamed and I stabbed it. I stabbed the Toy Monkey in the heart!

62

Beat.

BOFF   I'm sorry Kal. Your knife's still in him.

Beat.

KAL   He can keep it.

LOU   *(to **Boff**, hugging Richard)* You saved him!

JAZ   You were very brave.

*Beat. **Boff** looks coy.*

KAL   *(awkwardly)* Yeah. Well done.

*He slaps **Boff** on the back, a bit too hard. A man comes onstage, a **nightwatchman**.*

NIGHTWATCHMAN Oy!

The kids all jump.

NIGHTWATCHMAN What you kids doing here? This is Private Property.

BOFF   We, er, …

MAL   We're doing a Project!

NIGHTWATCHMAN Bit late for that kind of thing isn't it?

JAZ   It's, em, about Things That Go Bump In The Night.

LOU   I bet you get a lot of Night Bumps in your job!

NIGHTWATCHMAN I could tell you a thing or two.

BOFF	Do you know anything about this house?
NIGHTWATCHMAN	Oh yes. I've been keeping an eye on this place for nearly 30 years.
KAL	Can you tell us who it belongs to?
NIGHTWATCHMAN	Doesn't belong to anyone anymore. The guy who owned it died last night.

Beat.

KAL	Last night?
JAZ	What?!
RO	Did he ... Did he still live there?
NIGHTWATCHMAN	You must be joking. No one could live in there. It's a death trap. No. No he died in jail. He'd been there for years. *(scary voice)* People say he murdered his mother.
JAZ	What ... what would he do that for?
NIGHTWATCHMAN	She was cruel to him apparently. He was brought up on fear. She locked him in cupboards and burnt him with cigarettes. That sort of thing. And then one day, he turned. Apparently he had a pet monkey and she'd killed it.

Beat.

TILLY	That's horrible.
NIGHTWATCHMAN	Yes. Still. It's all in the past now eh? *(he moves away)* All in the past now.

He exits. The children look at each other for a moment, gobsmacked. Terrified they all run offstage as fast as they can.

Scene 13: Kal's bedroom

Kal, Mal, Ro, Tilly, Jaz and Boff are settling down in sleeping bags on the floor.

Ro	You could've let Lou sleep in your room after all that Kal!
Kal	No. She's not allowed. It's my sleepover. Not hers.

While they're talking, Lou runs on and settles down in her own sleeping bag outside the door.

Jaz	Come on Kal. Before you go to sleep. Tell us what you were scared of.
Kal	No.
Tilly	Oh *go* on Kally.
Kal	No.
Jaz	Let's see if we can guess it.
Mal	Yeah! Is it Ghosts Kally?
Kal	No.
Boff	Is it snakes?
Kal	No.
Ro	Spiders?
Kal	No!
Mal	Is it Zombies?
Kal	Go to sleep.

BOFF	Is it a person?
KAL	*(beat)* What?
JAZ	It is! It is! He didn't say no. It definitely is.
BOFF	Is it someone you know?
KAL	Look. It's not, alright. But if you really have to know a secret, I'll tell you that thing that Lou's scared of.

Lou's head bobs up out of her sleeping bag.

BOFF	You can't do that, you promised.
KAL	Well then, let's go to sleep shall we?
BOFF	*(beat)* Alright.

They turn off the lights.

MAL	*(after a moment)* Just whisper it to me Kally. I won't tell anyone.
LOU	I'm right outside the door Kal!

Kal sits bolt upright.

KAL	What?! I told you to go to bed!!
LOU	I'm not *in* the room, I'm outside. And I can hear every word you say. So you'd better not.
KAL	Go back to your room or I will.
LOU	No! I'm not even *in* the room. And if you tell them I'll tell Daddy.
KAL	Right. Here comes your first clue everybody.

Lou	I'll tell Daddy!!
Kal	*(donkey noises)* Eeyore! Eeyore! Eeeeeeeeeeeeeeeyoooooooooooore!!
Lou	*(wails)* I hate you!

Mayhem. **Mal** *laughs his head off,* **Ro** *and* **Tilly** *also laugh.* **Lou** *bursts into the room and jumps on* **Kal***, starts trying to beat him up.* **Kal** *responds.* **Boff** *tries to drag him off.* **Jaz** *tries to drag* **Lou** *off. A light comes on on the landing.*

Voice	*(offstage, loud)* What the Hell is going on in there!!!!

They all stop in their tracks.

Kal	Dad!

Everyone immediately assumes sleeping positions and starts to snore. A shadow looms onto the landing. The shadow is followed soon after by **The Man***. He stands on the landing and watches the children sleeping. Lights fade. End of play.*

Staging the play

THE SET-UP

Read the first scene of Judith Johnson's play very closely. It contains a lot of information that the audience needs to absorb to enjoy the whole play. In theatre, this sequence of dialogue and action is known as 'the set-up'. What the characters say literally sets up everything an audience needs to know to fully understand what is about to be played out. In this play, we meet the main characters, hear the style of the dialogue, understand the relationships between the main characters, and have an understanding of where the play is set (in and around a family house, in a small town which could be anywhere in the country). We also get a big hint about the plot as the haunted house and its sometime inhabitants are described in great detail. The characters' curiosities are aroused in such a way that the audience know (and wish) that they will go and explore this seemingly dangerous location.

Exercise

Make a very detailed list of all the information the audience gains from the first ten pages of the script. Include everything and anything, as you may find as you rehearse the play that it becomes in some way useful.

STATUS

The audience are introduced to all the main characters in this first scene. They also become aware of the status each

68

character has in relation to the others. All the main characters know each other very well when the play begins. The only character they don't know is the mysterious Man who will become the pivot of the drama later on. However, his character is introduced in this scene as Kal describes him in his story. This description will stay in the audience's mind and will start to feed their imagination before they actually see and hear him in the drama.

The status of each character is very clear in the script and you should make sure that the way the actors play these characters remains true to this from the outset. It is particularly important as the status of each character is going to be tested by events as they unfold. Kal clearly has highest status: he is a natural leader. By the end of the play, however, he has to face his fears and reveal an inner part of himself that he has kept hidden: his fear of his father. Boff has the lowest status yet with him the opposite happens: through his courage, his status is momentarily elevated in the final scenes.

CASTING

When casting your production, you should think carefully about the natural status of the actors who are available. The children's characters are all very realistic and it would make sense to cast the production making the most of qualities that your young actors have already. Think about who has the strongest presence, who is a natural leader, who prefers to 'play second fiddle' and who would be good to play someone who begins as being weak and ends up gaining strength through personal bravery. It is important to look at physical characteristics when casting as well as vocal and personality traits.

It is worth remembering that in good plays the status of characters shifts according to what is going on in the scene. For example, a character with mid-level status may become high status if the character with higher status leaves the stage. Actors and their director should think carefully about body language in each scene, and how subtle changes may occur according to which actors are present in the space.

The dialogue in *Scary Play* is very clear in delineating status. You should work carefully on the physicalisation of each character and situation in light of this. There are a lot of moments of suspense and tension in this play, primarily generated and controlled by the words and actions of The Man. However you will achieve a richer texture if you explore and present the internal tensions amongst the group of young adventurers, tensions that are usually rooted in status.

Status Game 1 Action

This game is all about an actor's action and what it imparts to the audience.

- An actor volunteers and chooses a playing card from a deck held face down by the director. If it is a high card – an ace, a king, etc – then he or she will play high status, if it is a low card – a 2 or 3 – then he or she will play low status. If it is around 4, 5 or 6 then they will play mid-status. The actor should not show anyone else the card.

- A chair is placed in the centre of the acting space. The chair has the status of 10.

- The actor must enter the space and play the status he or she has in relation to the chair. The audience must guess what status he or she is playing and when asked suggest numbers. Allow every actor in the company to have a go at this.

- See how accurately the audience can guess the status of the actor according to his or her body language. As you get more specific at this game, you'll be surprised at how accurately the audience is able to guess the right number.

Status Game 2 Improvisation

Now, replace the chair with another actor.

- Both actors have chosen cards. They have not told anyone the number of their status.

- They enter the space and are given a location which is a neutral public place, such as neighbouring seats on a plane or a long queue for tickets at a music gig. They are strangers who have never met before. As they begin to speak and become aware of each other's body language they may also become aware of each other's status.

- The improvisation must last no longer than five minutes, as it may become tedious. The audience's reports on what they absorb from what they see and hear are crucial. The actors will learn a lot from their feedback.

 DESIGN

Before deciding on how you are going to design your production you should think carefully of the configuration of your acting space. This play would work very well in any shaped auditorium.

There are three main locations that have to be shown:

A. Kal's bedroom, with a clear view of the other side of the bedroom door
B. Outside the house on Beech Street
C. The Man's bedroom/landing outside

A and C require a split acting area showing two separate locations of which only the audience has a full view. They should believe that the actors in each separate location can't see the actors in the other.

B is basically an open space with the suggestion of the house in the distance. As this location is revisited, the house becomes closer as the actors have to enter through the front door of the house, see a light at a window, and climb through one of the windows up a length of rope.

If you are using a pros arch or end-on stage then your split locations may look like the illustrations below:

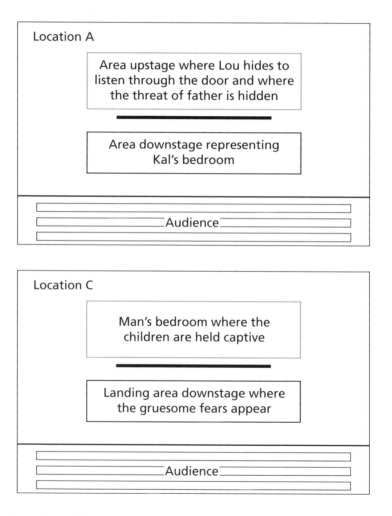

Fig 1: staging with a pros arch or end-on stage.

If you decide to stage your production in the round, the above theory applies but it would look like this:

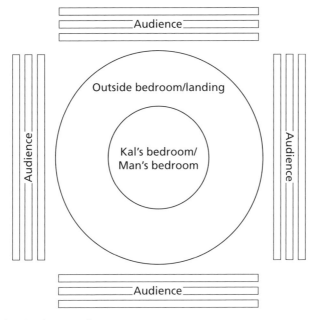

Fig 2 staging in the round.

If you were to stage *Scary Play* in a traverse setting where the audience sit on opposite sides of the acting space, you could establish the locations like this:

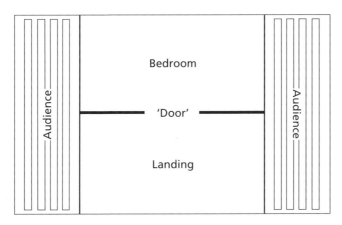

Fig 3 traverse staging.

For the scenes in Kal's bedroom, it would be better to use the central area of the stage, as this is where most of the action is focused, and to use one of the narrow sides of the acting area as the landing where Lou appears.

 DOORS

It seems necessary to have practical doors in this play: the door into Kal's bedroom, the front door of the haunted house, and also the door which separates the Man's bedroom from the landing where the clowns, coffin and vampires appear.

If you experiment with ways of suggesting that there is a door without actually having a door you will find neater ways of staging. You may find ways of showing where the door frame is, so that you can achieve the effect of Lou listening on the other side of the door. The audience can see her; the actors play the scene as if they cannot.

The only door you may find it actually necessary to have is the door which leads into the haunted house, as the actors in this scene need a focal point and there is the business of the door seemingly opening and closing itself.

FURNITURE AND FURNISHINGS

When delineating the space of the rooms, you may find that using one piece of furniture is sufficient. The most obvious choice would be a bed, which can be re-dressed to double as Kal's bed and The Man's bed. If you are staging in the round or traverse you may find that a large rug is enough to represent the floor area of each bedroom with the empty floor of the acting area around them representing the outdoor space. If you choose this option, go for two contrasting rugs to represent the insides of the two different houses.

The key to concentrating attention on the actors and story, and achieving swift transitions from one location to another, is 'less is more'. Choose one or two strong pieces in your design concept and the dialogue coupled with the audience's imagination will do the rest.

Always start with the play text for the chief clues about how the production will look. Kal's description of the house on Beech Street is quite detailed:

KAL   It was all sort of, broken up inside. The floorboards were rotting, the wallpaper was peeling, it reeked of piss, there were blood stains on the walls and the furniture was falling to pieces.

Scour the script for as many clues as you can, making notes on a sheet of paper or drawing quick sketches before you start designing the production. That way you will avoid missing out important features as you arrive at your final design concept.

COSTUMES

The children characters wear pyjamas and football kits. They then put on coats and shoes. These should be easy to move in and to put on quickly. You should use elastic instead of shoe laces so they can be ready tied and pulled onto the feet.

The monkey's costume is a special challenge. You may find someone who is able to make it out of fake fur. Or you may be able to adapt an existing brown or red suit and add a monkey mask.

Remember to give the monkey a tail which the actor will be able to play with. You will also need to find a white dentist's coat which can fit over the monkey outfit.

For the costume which The Man wears, you may find a suit in a charity shop. You should distress it so it looks well worn.

It would be good if the Nightwatchman's face were obscured by large scarf or dark glasses or peaked cap. You may decide to dress him in security uniform, for example a bright yellow reflective jacket.

Costume ideas for the scary characters who appear on the landing:

Vampire:

Clowns:

Scary Clown Make-Up:

 PROPS

You should make the knife safe by blunting the blade. Actors should take great care when using props like this and actions should be meticulously rehearsed.

The axe should look real but not be as heavy as a real axe (although the actor should act as though it is). You may need a second duplicate axe as later on there is a moment when the axe head falls off and drops to the floor. In one scene, there is broken glass on the floor. You should use pieces of clear plastic with the edges sanded so they are not sharp. If it is heavy duty plastic it should still make the noise of broken glass being swept up.

See if you can find an X-ray vision spy head set in a toyshop. Or you may be able to find a photograph of one online or in a catalogue and replicate it by adapting a large pair of sunglasses or plastic shades.

The dentist's chair is an important prop. Have a look at this photograph of an old fashioned dentist's chair and adapt an old chair on wheels so that it looks like one.

Squeaky wheels: they could either be really squeaky or this could be a sound effect, live or recorded.

Plastic hygiene gloves are available to buy from chemists but you may be able to ask a local nurse or your school kitchen to give you a couple of pairs as they are sold in bulk. Ask a local chemist or doctors surgery for a large plastic syringe. Don't use a needle as this would be too dangerous. Have a power drill but don't power it up – use a sound effect for the drill to make a noise.

Another important prop is the coffin on wheels. Ask your local undertakers if they have a display model you could borrow for your production. The dead mother inside could be a puppet which is operated by the monkey or perhaps rigged to the lid so that when the lid is opened the 'mother' is seen to sit up and shoot out her arm.

LIGHTING

The play begins with the actors using six hand held torches. Get good strong-beam ones, with reliable switches and batteries.

Outside perhaps use a special to show the moon – it could be a full moon. Scary stories often happen in moonlight and it will also serve as a constant reminder that all events in this play happen at night. If budget allows, perhaps you could buy a glass moon gobo like the one on the left. If projected onto a simple white disc hung high at the back of the stage, it gives a good impression of a real moon. There could also be stars in a black back cloth to show that it is the night sky. These could easily then be switched off when the action moves indoors.

You will want to cross-fade the lighting in the split stage sequences. So have the lighting up full on the Man's bedroom, and then fade it to 30% or to a purple/blue state to show that the focus has switched, whilst bringing up the lights to an eerie full state on the area of stage that represents the landing.

SOUND

When the explorers go into the house, their voices are heard to echo. These echoes could be pre-recorded or created by other actors offstage. If you yell into a large metal dustbin or similar vessel you should get the desired effect.

On page 26 there is a sound that makes them all jump. What could this sound be? How could you create it? It should be loud and sharp and short. You need to be able to play or make it so that it occurs accurately on cue.

MUSIC

Music is required to accompany the sequences on the landing. You need to find some scary fairground music and also some sinister music to accompany the vampires. This could be pre-recorded; you may be able to download it. You may even be able to distort some existing music using an editing kit which will give it the required sinister effect. The music in your production could be played live on a keyboard with different instrument effects programmed: for example, a fairground organ or church organ. If the music is played live you will be able to time it to the action much more easily. Make sure that whoever is playing the keyboard has a clear view of the acting space and the actors.

You may find that additional scary music is useful for scene shifts. Think of the music as marking the end of one scene and introducing the next rather than it being a piece of music to cover a scene change. This will ensure that the pace of the production stays slick and that no music is used unnecessarily.

On page 57, the choice of music to bring all the scary characters back on is crucial. It could be a piece of music of which snippets have been used all the way through. Listen to the grand choral music of classical composers like Gluck. Church music can be sinister. The sound of a large church organ would be good to accompany the arrival of the coffin. Choirs singing anthems in Latin would also work well in these sequences.

SPECIAL EFFECTS

- When the characters enter the haunted house, Judith Johnson suggests that rats scuttle across the floor – you could achieve this with lighting and sound effects.

- Don't really tie the actors to furniture, use ropes which are knotted and look as though they are tied but in fact the actors can easily be freed. This is useful for scene changes and keeping the action nippy. You could use elastic or Velcro along with the rope which is pre-knotted in order that the binding can easily be slipped onto the actors.

Have a close look at the names of the children. What are the names short for? Kal rhymes with Mal. Kal sounds stronger, why is this?

Exercise

Ask each actor in turn to describe, in role, what their character typically does on a Sunday afternoon. They should include detail about all their family members, the place where they live, the local area, any pets they might have, meals they share and places they might visit.

🎭 ACTING

- The stakes are often high for all the protagonists in this play. Once inside the house, characters are continually reacting and responding to events, to things that happen to them or other people. Subconsciously the audience will be going through the same experience, thinking: "What if it was me tied-up in that room?"; "What is my secret fear?".

- Actors should avoid playing a generalised fear. All actors should be very specific when playing reactions, and it is crucial that the scary scenes are played for truth as otherwise they will seem silly. There is a good book, called *The Actor and the Target* by Declan Donnellan, which explains lots of exercises actors can try to help them achieve truth in acting.

- Unspoken thoughts: remember there are always moments when characters don't say what they are thinking. Actors must allow time to elapse and actually undergo the thought processes each time they play the scene otherwise it will not have any truth.

Playing intention is also crucial in *Scary Play*. Read this extract from Scene Five:

TILLY	Is this your house? Our friends came in here. They didn't mean to trespass or nothing. It was just for fun.
THE MAN	Ah. Fun. I see.
RO	*(trembling)* They didn't mean any harm. Please let them out. We all just want to go home. Don't we Tilly?
THE MAN	You think I've got your friends in that room?

Beat.

RO	Yes.
TILLY	No!

Why does RO say 'yes' and TILLY say 'no' simultaneously? Do they have the same intention? Or are their intentions opposite?

What unspoken thoughts do all three characters have during the '*Beat*' (a short pause in the rhythm of the dialogue)?

A useful exercise to explore a character's intention is to ask each actor to say what their intention is before saying the line. As an example, the intentions for this scene are given in bold print:

TILLY	**Make a good impression on The Man so he won't harm them** Is this your house? Our friends came in here. They didn't mean to trespass or nothing. It was just for fun.
THE MAN	**Show he has highest status** Ah. **Show Tilly and Ro that he doesn't believe it was just for fun.** Fun. **Intimidate them** I see.
RO	**Persuade The Man to let them go free** *(trembling)* They didn't mean any harm. Please let them out. We all just want to go home. **Have run out of ideas for things to say, turns to Tilly for support** Don't we Tilly?
THE MAN	**Tease them** You think I've got your friends in that room?

Be specific in the playing of every single line. Remember it is impossible to play an internal 'feeling'. Instead you must show the outside manifestation of that feeling, whether it reveals itself in the sound of the voice, the overall physicality of the body, or in your relationship to another character or the surroundings.

❪❩❪❩ TEXT RHYTHM

The Man probably has a different speech rhythm to the children. His voice is older and he will show his maturity by sounding calmer. In the circumstances this will make him more sinister as it will contrast with the apparent naivety of the children.

The monkey doesn't have any lines to speak. His part is silent. His actions therefore need to be very specific, and should not be exaggerated or played for comic effect. If you are fortunate enough to live near a zoo, it would be worth visiting the monkey enclosure to study the animals' movements. Alternatively, you could get hold of film footage of monkeys for the actor playing the monkey to watch so that he or she can imitate their movements accurately. The actor should think as much about how the monkey will move as how he or she will sit still. Look closely at where the monkey holds their weight when sitting or standing.

Around the play

SCARY LOCATION

Drama

Split the company into two groups. Each group has a different room to use.

They must create a scary place and then invite the others inside to explore.

Creative writing

Working in pairs, one actor is blindfolded and guided around a room. As the blindfolded partners touch and smell things, they should use their imagination and describe what they think is there if they could see. The guide then writes it all down on a pad.

Storyboarding

Choose one character. In comic strip form, storyboard the nightmare they would have about their fear.

Can you think of other current slang sayings which you hear among young people? Do they have actions that go with them? Where do you think they originate from? Are they purely comic or do they have a sinister side?

Slang actions

You may find that you're not familiar with some phrases and accompanying actions. For example: "Your Mum Works In McDonald's", "Your Mother's a Minger" (p.18) and "Loser Loser, Double Loser, Take a Picture. Look at Minger" (p.55).

All of these are hand movements. The first two involve making an "M" with thumbs and forefingers and swinging this round to form a "W" and then turning it back down as the "M". The same "M" symbol is used for "Minger". The final one involves making an "L" with thumb and forefinger with one hand and then the other, these then come together and are brought down to do a camera action and the "M" for "Minger" sign.

Storyboard these words and actions in cartoon style.

Discussion Point

Why does this last saying become funny and sinister when The Man says it towards the end of the play?

PLAYING GAMES

"Spin the bottle" is a party game in which several players sit in a circle. The game starts by one player spinning a bottle. The spinner must kiss whomever the bottle points to or give them a dare. The person being kissed or performing the dare becomes the next spinner.

- Which other games played by children can you think of?

- What are the risks?

- Why are they fun and exciting?

Creative Writing

Write a short story in which a dare gets out of hand and leads to big trouble.

THOUGHT-TRACKING

- Choose one of the children characters.

- Read the play very carefully from his or her point of view.

- As you get to your character's lines, read them aloud.

- Every time your character has a new thought, write it down.

- You may find it interesting to track all the characters' thoughts and map them along the wall on a long frieze.

WORDS AND EXPRESSIONS

Have a good look at the photograph on the previous page from a production of *Scary Play*.

It is from the scene when the young adventurers see the haunted house on Beech Street for the first time. Write as many words as you can think of which describe the expressions on their faces.

Straitjacket

This is a photograph of a straitjacket.

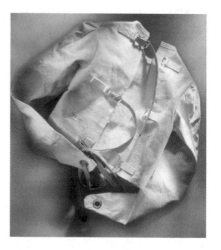

See if you can find out when they were first used and who invented them.

What are they used for today?

How do they work?

What are they made from?

How easy is it to escape from a straitjacket?

Research: MI5

Lou aspires to be a spy. She certainly has all the right equipment packed in her rucksack and is quick to take anything along on an expedition that she thinks might be useful. At one moment in the script she mentions MI5 – what is this organisation? Find out as much as you can about it by asking relatives and looking in books and online. Write a brief outline of the organisation's history and activities. You may find it useful to look at their website: www.mi5.gov.uk.

Make a list of spy films and famous spy characters from fiction.

Sidling Ribaldry

Lou sometimes gets her words mixed up. When she talks of sidling ribaldry on page 26 she means sibling rivalry. This play demonstrates what happens when an older brother bullies his younger sister.

You should write Lou's diary as if you were Lou. It would not be written from a glum, low-status, victim point of view because Lou has a plucky outlook and big ambitions to become a super-detective and explorer.

Animals Real and Imaginary

Discussion

Here is a question for the whole company to discuss: what is the overall effect of there being a toy dog and a real monkey in this play?

Richard the dog is a stuffed toy. He was bought for Lou for Christmas by Kal. She treasures Richard, talking to him as if he were another member of the group and asking advice of him.

The Man talks to his monkey. The monkey is seemingly real and seems to be unloved.

What extra dimension does the inclusion of these animal characters give to this story?

SUSPENSE

There are many sequences in this play which create intense suspense. Read this scene aloud including the stage directions. Think carefully about timing and pause where necessary.

A torch light shines in the upstairs window. They both see it.

Lou   What's that light?

Boff   What light?

The light shines again.

Lou   That light.

Boff   Er …

Lou   I thought you said they hadn't gone in?

*Beat. The door swings open with a creak. Pause. **Lou** looks at **Boff**.*

Lou   I thought you said the door was locked.

Boff   Please don't go in there Lou.

Lou   You come in too if you're worried about me.

Boff   I'm, er, on Look Out.

Lou   Look out for what? The scary stuff's in there
                   isn't it? Not out here.

Boff   No but … there might be police coming. Or
                   something. Or your Dad! So I need to …
                   look out.

Lou   You're going to let me go in by myself aren't
                   you?

*Pause. **Boff** looks away. **Lou** shakes her head sadly.*

Lou   See ya Boff.

***Lou** goes in to the house, possibly sidling like a spy along the wall on
the way in. She picks up the axe left earlier by **Mal**. The door swings
shut behind her.*

STATUS SHIFTS

Look carefully at the sequence of scenes inside The Man's bedroom. Kal is very frustrated when Mal succumbs to The Man. Until this point Kal has been the leader and he suddenly finds that he has lost power over the group. Power seems to shift from Kal to The Man. Eventually there is a much greater turning point, when Kal admits to his fears.

DESCRIBING ACTION

Whilst writing *Scary Play*, Judith Johnson was reading a lot of Darren Shan books with her young son. This is how she describes his stories:

> Darren Shan's vampire chronicles are a psychological masterpiece if you read them from start to finish. One boy's struggle to cope with being different and entering

into a world of fear and shame only to emerge triumphant
and also on the moral high-ground at the end!

There are many Darren Shan horror books available: have a
look in your local bookshop or in your library.

Read this extract from Darren Shan's *Hunters of the Dusk:
Vampires at War*:

Before I could say anything else, he darted forward,
seized me by the throat and made a small, painful cut
across my neck with his nails.

"Ow!" I yelled, stumbling away from him.

"Next time I'll cut your nose off," he said pleasantly.

"No you won't!" I growled and swung at him with
my sword, properly this time.

Vancha ducked clear of the arc of the blade. "Good,"
he grinned. "That's more like it."

He circled me, eyes on mine, fingers flexing slowly.
I kept the tip of my sword low, until he came to a halt,
then moved towards him and jabbed. I expected him
to shift aside, but instead he brought the palm of his
right hand up and swiped the blade away, as he would
a flat stick. As I struggled to bring it back around, he
stepped in, caught hold of my hand above the wrist,
gave a sharp twist which caused me to release the
sword – and I was weaponless.

"See?" he smiled, stepping back and raising his
hands to show the fight was at an end. "If this was for
real, your ass would be grass." Vancha had a foul
mouth – that was one of his tamest insults!

"Big deal," I sulked, rubbing my sore wrist. "You
beat a half-vampire. You couldn't win against a full-
vampire or a vampaneze."

"I can and have," he insisted. "Weapons are tools of fear, used by those who are afraid. One who learns to fight with his hands always has the advantage over those who rely on swords and knives. Know why?"

"Why?"

"Because they expect to win," he beamed. "Weapons are false – they're not of nature – and inspire false confidence. When I fight, I expect to die. Even now, when I sparred with you, I anticipated death and resigned myself to it. Death is the worst this world can throw at you, Darren – if you accept it, it has no power over you."

Picking up my sword, he handed it to me and watched to see what I'd do. I had the feeling he wanted me to cast it aside – and I was tempted to, to earn my respect. But I'd have felt naked without it, so I slid it back into its sheath and glanced down at the ground, slightly ashamed.

Vancha clasped the back of my neck and squeezed amiably. "Don't let it bother you," he said. "You're young. You have loads of time to learn." His eyes creased as he thought about Mr Tiny and the Lord of the Vampaneze, and he added gloomily, "I hope."

The actions in this section of the book are described in great detail. The writer is careful to describe them accurately so that the reader or listener can develop a visual picture of what is happening. The writer is also economical and stylish in his choice of words and phrases. This prevents the description becoming tedious and boring. You may notice that there are a lot of verbs in the extract: flexing, squeezed, swiped, slid, clasped, seized, jabbed. Verbs are doing words. Using them instead of adjectives makes the text fast-paced and dynamic.

Writing

Write your own description of a fight scene. Make it as complicated and detailed as you like but also be imaginative in the way you use language so that it is always stylish and exciting for the reader or listener.

THE MAN'S CHILDHOOD

Exercise set by Judith Johnson

Imagine you are The Man aged 10. Imagine what your favourite place in your house is. It could be a room, it could be a particular place to sit, it could even be under your bed. Now write a detailed description of that place: what it looks like, how it feels to be there, why you like it so much. Or draw a detailed picture of it.

Now, still as The Man aged 10, what is your least favourite place in the house? Again, write a detailed description or draw a picture showing how horrible that place is to you and why you hate it so much.

SEQUEL

When the children are all safely back in Kal's bedroom, who is the man who appears at the very end of the play? His appearance suggests that perhaps the story is not over.

Write the sequel to this play and design the poster for a production. You may write it as a short story with illustrations or you may want to write it as a drama with dialogue and actions for all the characters. Alternatively you could write it as a film or a radio play. Call it *Scary Play 2*.